Tungula's Gift

Tungula's Gift

LUIS ABELARDO NÚÑEZ

Translated from Spanish by
Ada and Roger Fidler

FIDLERHOUSE
Columbia, Missouri

Library of Congress Control Number: Pending
ISBN: 978-1-6953-6324-3

This book also is available from Amazon.com
as a Kindle e-book.

To the reasons for my life ...

I dedicate this book, witness of my dreams and the boat on which my memories sail, to my beautiful Ferreñafe — its legends, history, and traditions — and to all the people who love peace and justice.

With emotion, love, and gratitude for the three Núñez Delgado sisters, born in Ferreñafe under the dazzling sun of Lambayeque. Tarcila de Takahashi, my unforgettable mother who gave me her benediction before she began her trip to heaven. She left when she was in the flower of her existence.

To my remembered aunts: Virginia de Kanno, anonymous and sacrificing heroine, modest woman but gigantic in her tenderness; and Etelvina de Itabashi who was my loving teacher of guitar and theater. She left me on a full stage where I am an actor in the eternal work — dreams of Life and Death.

To my four siblings: Amanda, Jorge, Soledad, and Blanca Takahashi Núñez.

To my self-sacrificing wife, Maria Nila Bautista Palacios, and my seven unique children: Cristina Tarcila, Luisa Elizabeth, María Nila, Lourdes Rossana, Luis Abelardo, Katty Adela, and Pedro Leonardo.

About the Author

Luis Abelardo Núñez is one of the most revered Peruvian composers and writers of his generation. Abelardo, as he was called by those who knew him and appreciated his music and short stories, was born in Ferreñafe, a small farming village near Chiclayo in northern Peru, on November 22, 1926.

His father, Sakuzo Takahashi, immigrated to Peru from Fukushima, Japan. His mother, Tarcila Núñez Delgado, was Peruvian. Both parents died when he was very young. His aunt Virginia de Kanno, who was a seamstress and the wife of a Japanese barber in Ferreñafe, took over the responsibility for rearing him and his four other orphaned siblings.

From an early age, Abelardo was enthralled by the music and folklore of northern Peru. With the guidance of another aunt, Etelvina de Itabashi, he learned to play guitar and other instruments as well as to write and compose songs. When he was 19 years old, he moved to Lima, the capital of Peru, to pursue his musical career. To be accepted as a Peruvian musician and composer, he adopted his mother's family name — Núñez.

Abelardo composed and wrote lyrics for more than 200 songs in a wide variety of styles. He became known as "The Composer of the People" because of his strong connection with the populace and his selfless support in the struggle for social justice. He had a genuine affection for all of the people and lands of his mother country. But it was his beloved Ferreñafe, where the pre-Inca Sicán people constructed the pyramids at Batán Grande, that always possessed his heart and soul.

Abelardo and his wife Nila (María Nila Bautista Palacios) moved to Nagoya, Japan, in 1996 to be with their children who had decided earlier that year to emigrate from Peru to the native country of their grandfather. On December 19, 2005, Abelardo died in Japan after a long battle with melanoma. His body was returned to Peru for burial in Ferreñafe.

Contents

Foreword

Tungula's Gift is the last short story written by Luis Abelardo Núñez, and the first to be translated from Spanish into English. In this story, Abelardo blends the legends and mysteries of the Sicán people, who established an enduring, sophisticated culture in northern Peru long before the Spanish conquest, with his magical experiences as a young boy in 1937 on a journey from his home in Ferreñafe to the hacienda at Batán Grande.

In addition to building enormous complexes of pyramids and extensive irrigation systems, the Sicán people created fine textiles, intricate gold and silver ornaments, and many distinctive types of pottery. One form, called a huaco silbador [whistling vessel], plays a central role in Abelardo's tale.

The backstory of how we came to publish **Tungula's Gift** as a paperback book and Amazon Kindle edition, began on January 18, 1985, at a radio station in Lima, Peru. After Ada Vigo sang several of Abelardo's songs during the annual Day of Lima celebration, the composer introduced himself and invited her to sing at a concert he was preparing to give at the Municipal Theater. At the time, she was a reporter for *El Comercio*, Peru's most important newspaper. While Peruvian music was her passion and she had been singing Abelardo's songs for many years, she had never sung professionally or in front of a large audience. Initially, she was hesitant to accept his invitation, but Abelardo prevailed. From that chance meeting, a friendship flourished that would radically change her life and mine.

In September 1987, the InterAmerican Press Association invited me to speak about my work in digital publishing at a technology conference hosted by *El Comercio* in Lima. I didn't speak Spanish then and this was my first visit to a South American country. The editor of the paper knew that Ada was fluent in English, so he assigned her to translate my presentation and to be my guide. He told her to "take good care of Mr. Fidler and make sure he has a good impression of Peru."

She followed his instructions so well that eighteen months later we were married in Miami, and Peru still is my favorite country to visit. We have come to believe that Abelardo had a hand in all of this, but that's another story.

My first opportunity to meet Abelardo in person came in April 1998. He was visiting his relatives in New Jersey while I was in New York to speak at a Columbia University symposium.

Ada and I offered to take him with us to the Big Apple for a few days. He was eager to explore the city but also wanted to attend the symposium. The topic was the future of publishing. After my presentation, he could hardly contain his excitement. The notion that stories could be published electronically and read immediately by people almost anywhere in the world captivated Abelardo.

Through Ada, he asked if I could produce a digital edition of a book he was writing. Always a cultural ambassador for Peru, he thought this would be a great way for people to know more about his country's rich traditions and history. I told him if that was his wish, I would be happy to do it for free.

In December 2002, we traveled to Ferreñafe to be with Abelardo when the city where he was born and began his musical career honored him as its "Favorite Son." During that visit, he told his nephew to take us to the Sicán complex at Batán Grande. He indicated that this was the subject of the story that I had promised to publish as an electronic book.

Before we left Ferreñafe, Abelardo said he would send us his manuscript as soon as it was finished. Two years later, he was diagnosed with a melanoma that soon spread to his brain.

After his death in December 2005, his wife Nila told us that in his final days he frequently reminded her to send us his manuscript for the digital edition. But, in the turmoil of that stressful time, it became misplaced among all of his papers. We finally received the manuscript in the fall of 2006. The following year, we created a digital version in English and Spanish using Adobe's PDF software. It was briefly posted on a Peruvian website dedicated to Abelardo.

When I retired from the Missouri School of Journalism in January 2015, we established FIDLERHOUSE to provide services for authors who want to self-publish their manuscripts. That May, we formally purchased from Nila all rights to *Tungula's Gift* and all of Abelardo's other unpublished works. With her encouragement, we reformatted the book in 2019 for reading on the Amazon Kindle e-readers and mobile media apps and produced this paperback edition, which can be purchased through Amazon and other booksellers. — ROGER FIDLER

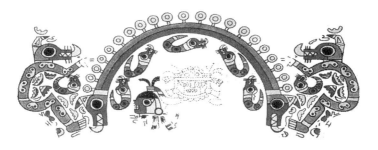

Introduction

Contemplating the high summits of the mountain range of the Pacific, the mind of man portrays the Andean landscapes. An intimate voice disturbs and wraps us in a fog of mystery and dreams. Perhaps this is the reason why the *ferreñafanos* [residents of Ferreñafe] are slaves to incredible legends.

The province of Ferreñafe in the department of Lambayeque contains evidence of many ancient cultures that date back to about 500 BC. However, it is the people who built the enormous complexes at Batán Grande and Tucume in the Río de la Leche [Milk River] Valley between the years 800 and 1300 AD that have captivated Peruvians and scholars from around the world.

The name given to these people and their culture is Sicán, which means "House of the Moon" in the ancient Muchik language. Archaeologists believe they probably are descendants of the Moche.

The population included many highly skilled artisans and metal workers as is evidenced by the vast quantities of gold, silver, and

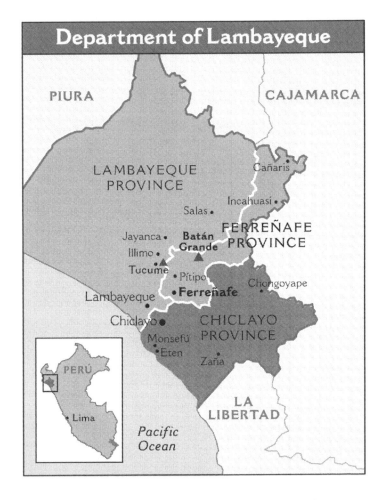

copper artifacts found in the Sicán tombs. They knew the secrets for producing delicate gold ornaments and an arsenic-copper alloy, which is the closest material to bronze found in pre-Columbian America. According to Julio C. Tello, the father of Peruvian archaeology, nearly all of the gold and silver extracted by the people of South America in prehistoric times came from northern Peru, and at least three quarters of the archaeological specimens of Peruvian gold that exist in foreign and national museums came from the department of Lambayeque, mainly from the archaeological nucleus of Batán Grande and Túcume.

The Sicán population also included people who knew the secrets of medicinal herbs, and produced fine textiles and sophisticated pottery. Among the types of pottery that they created there was a musical instrument similar to a flute, which could take many shapes and acquire many different sounds, called a huaco silbador [whistling vessel].

Around 1100 AD, the Batán Grande complex with its 20 pyramids was abandoned, probably because of a great flood that damaged the irrigation channels and agricultural lands. The Sicán people soon established a new religious and ceremonial center at Tucume. The culture flourished for another two centuries until a great drought that lasted for more than 30 years brought about its rapid collapse.

The Sicán people were eventually conquered in about 1350 AD by the kingdom of the Great Chimú, which encompassed all of the modern department of Lambayeque. The old chronicles say that about one hundred years before the Spanish conquest of Peru in the sixteenth century, the Inca Huayna Capac occupied the Chimú kingdom. The Penachí tribe resisted and was never totally subdued. The territory of these brave rebels probably reached into what is now the province of Ferreñafe.

The Batán Grande Estate

The opportunity should not be passed up to add some notes about the Batán Grande estate, inside whose boundaries was the Batán Grande complex. The Spanish archives show that in the year 1527 Don Francisco de Barbarán bought the lands, mounds, tombs and idols from the cacique [native overlord] of Illimo. The estate subsequently passed to Juan de Barbarán, who sold it in the year 1612 to Don Antonio de Villavicencio. The earliest recorded name given to the property was San Nicolás de Sicán or Cicán.

The Batán Grande estate house circa 1940.

At the beginning of the nineteenth century, the owner of the estate was Don Andrés Delgado. He is said to have planted two mango trees from India, one of which still survived at the estate in 1970, according to Carlos Bachman's monograph about

Lambayeque. These trees at Batán Grande are believed to be the ancestors of all existing mango trees in Peru and Ecuador.

By the 1860s the property had become known as the Batán Grande hacienda. In 1913, Don Juan J. Aurich Pastor bought the property from the Delgado heirs. About 400 people resided at the estate in the 1920s. Upon his death in 1935, his children, the Aurich Bonilla, took possession. They continued to own and administer the estate until 1968 when they were forced out during the so-called "agrarian reformation."

View of the Pomac Forest Historic Sanctuary from one of the pyramids.

After years of neglect, the Peruvian government took a small step in 1984 to protect the property as an archaeological reserve. In 1991, it became known as the Batán Grande Reserve, and in 2001, the reserve was designated as the Pomac Forest Historic Sanctuary. The government is now making a greater effort to preserve the archaeological sites and the surrounding algarrobo forest that is one of two equatorial desert forests in the world.

Tungula, Almost a God

No one knows with absolute certainty the birthplace of Tungula, the great cacique who governed for many years that region where the eagles fly, the algarrobo [carob] trees flourish, the huerequeque bird sings, the foxes trifle, and the clay huacos whistle. Perhaps it was in Cañaris or Incahuasi where he saw his first light. What is most probable is that his children were born in Batán Grande.

The legends say that Tungula was a wise and noble lord. His beautiful wife Kalina is said to have possessed a magisterial and sweet voice that was like the songbirds of the paradise called Sicán. Their four children were the joy and happiness of these respected leaders of this region.

On nights when the moon was full, the Tungula family would ascend Chaparrí Hill; all wore resplendent clothing and crowns of gold inlaid with pearls and rare stones. Together with their subjects in that yunga chapel, they would offer strange prayers to an unknown god as they contemplated the clear and starry sky of Batán Grande.

Their eldest child, Amusuy, was a princess who dazzled everyone in that region. She was beautiful and generous to the people of her town. She also domesticated all the wild animals that lived in the Sicán territory. Her three brothers — Janque, Mollán and Puchaca — were master goldsmiths and good potters.

Tungula devoted his time to molding whistling huacos. He knew all the secrets of nature. From time to time he would travel to Penachí where he gathered miraculous herbs that he used for his healing rituals. All the townspeople knew about Tungula's strange powers and his ability to soften the hardest stones with his hands using tiny leaves of dark red color.

Tungula's ambition was to capture the voice of his beloved wife. One night he asked the god of the wind to grant him his wish. The next day, when Kalina tried to intone a prayer, she realized she had lost her voice. From that moment, all the whistling huacos made by Tungula acquired the musical and sonorous charm that subdues and bewitches.

Each son was given a whistling huaco created by this great lord. All were decorated with small heads of foxes. Janque received a huaco with two foxes, Mollán with three, and Puchaca with four, in that order. The huaco he gave to his daughter Amusuy was different; it was decorated with the small head of a parrot.

When Tungula delivered these fantastic huacos, he told his children that when he died they should bury him with all his best clothing and ornaments. That same should occur when his offspring left this world; the town had to bury them with all their most prized possessions and, of course, with their whistling huacos, so that Mother Earth will receive everything she has given us.

When Kalina saw that her husband was near death, she begged him to tell her the source of that fabulous leaf he used to soften stones; but already it was written that Tungula would carry to his tomb the secret that only is known by the sun, the wind, the rocks, the rain, and perhaps the birds that bring in their beaks the mysterious leaves whose sap is dark red like the yunga blood.

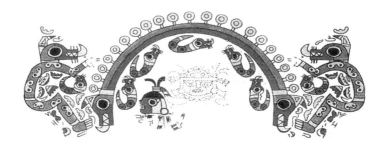

CHAPTER ONE
The Road to Batán Grande

The early morning was hot on the last Friday of February in the year 1937. The previous night it had rained torrentially. At the break of dawn, large heavy raindrops continued falling. The streets that ran in straight lines through the town of Ferreñafe had been converted into small streams. Murky water flowed along the cobblestones and kissed the curbs of the narrow paths paved with cement.

Small toads were hopping about; some managed to enter the houses. Wide-open doors facilitated the entry of those tiny friends of the farmers. Gigantic dragonflies of emerald green color perched on the high adobe walls covered with a plaster of gypsum and lime. This was an unmistakable sign of summer approaching and the time for sowing rice.

"Was it not a strong rainstorm, neighbor?" Don Jacinto inquired of an old farmer.

"Yes," answered the sower of rice, "but the water arrives late."

"Better late than never," Don Jacinto retorted.

That morning the housewives sought bread for breakfast. During those days the people of Ferreñafe could not imagine drinking a good cup of coffee with milk without their local bread greased with fresh butter from Monsefú or tasty mountain cheese produced in Sangana.

"Where did you get bread, comadre Luisa?"

"It's not bread, comadre. What I carry in my basket are yucas."

Because of the rains, the firewood was wet and the ovens were cold. The bakers had not thought ahead, which is why the town resorted to yucas, bananas, and sweet potatoes.

The whistle of the train could be heard clearly in the Plaza de Armas, which was six blocks away from the railway station. Travelers hurried their steps to arrive in time to find good seats. The train would leave at seven o'clock sharp bound for the port of Eten, passing through Lambayeque, Chiclayo, and Monsefú, the city of flowers and land of industrious people where women weave beautiful saddlebags of thread and hats of reeds. They also could prepare tasty snacks and good chicha [corn liquor] sweetened with honey.

Seven tolls of a bell marked the exact hour, the inexorable time that never stops. A turkey buzzard frolicked lazily on the cross atop the tower of the beautiful and ancient church of Santa

Lucía of Ferreñafe, founded in the year 1550. The sun king heated with his luminous rays the fertile and generous land.

The Journey Begins

On Unión Street the old truck of the Batán Grande estate, "Don Juan," was parked in a puddle of murky water. This morning the vehicle would transport several field workers along with some small-time merchants carrying their wares who expected to profit from the fortnight payday at the estate.

The body of "Don Juan" was soaked; the rain had left it in misery. As the sun continued to warm the morning, some passengers began boarding the vehicle. "Patuco," the assistant to the driver of the famous "Don Juan," took the crank and began turning it to activate the dynamo. The motor struggled several times before it finally started. All the passengers rejoiced as thick smoke escaped from the muffler.

Along the same Unión street lived a Japanese man named Kanno. This honest and industrious oriental had a barbershop. His companion and wife was a modest woman of Ferreñafe called Virginia. This seamstress, known by all as "Tía Vige" [Aunt Vige], was recognized for her generosity and kindness, which she demonstrated on different occasions.

For example, she often came to the aid of local poor people and even helped a few outsiders. These last mentioned were ones detained for brawling and did not have a bite to eat. After remaining for several days in the tiny jail of the civil guard, the food they received from Tía Vige was like a gift from heaven.

From the house of the Japanese, their nephew "Cholo" left hastily. The boy carried two cardboard boxes filled with clothing, the modest creations of his aunt Vige, which would be sold at the great estate of Batán Grande.

Cholo was in his eleventh year. Like all young boys, he was restless, but people noted that he was intelligent and because of his good behavior they liked him. In his neighborhood he was one of the best players on the soccer team that he baptized as "Estrella Roja" [Red Star]. Those were the days of the cloth soccer balls, when people talked about Lolo Fernández the "Striker," the "Magician" Valdiviezo, and Alejandro "Hose" Villanueva, stars of Peruvian soccer.

Cholo wore brand new overalls of bluish color. In the nickel-plated clasps were reflected the rays of the sun that peaked through Las Tres Tomas hill.

When the driver of the truck arrived, all greeted him with respect. This chauffeur knew all the defects and virtues of the famous small truck. "Don Juan Barbón," as they called this professional at the helm, was a tall white man with clear eyes who enjoyed good food and good liquor. He sang and danced the marinera gracefully. The Aurich family, owners of the Batán Grande estate, had great appreciation for him.

When Barbón took the wheel of the truck and lit his cigar, Tía Vige appeared. She was carrying a large battered suitcase that had seen better days. It was easy to see that it was heavy. As soon as she could, she handed it to Patuco. Then she went back to her house. When she returned to the truck, she carried in her right hand a steaming roasted sweet potato of purple color that she gave to her nephew Cholo. She then climbed up and accommodated herself in the cab of the dear old "Don Juan," the vehicle that had had a long history of love and sacrifice.

The Bridge to the Alameda

On the Carmona Bridge, which spans a large irrigation ditch and gives way to the romantic alameda, many people were waiting impatiently to travel to the estate. It was Friday. Saturday would be the fortnight payday and the town would have money. The Aurich family always paid on time. For that reason, they were respected and appreciated.

All sorts of baskets and containers of merchandise were accommodated on the platform of the truck. Who was most enthusiastic was Don Sevilla, the harness maker, who brought saddles, stirrups with silver corners, headstalls, bridles and reins. His products were sought after at the estate, and Don Sevilla could not keep from rubbing his hands and smiling at everyone.

"Hello Tía Vige! Are you also traveling to the estate?" Manuel inquired.

"No, I go to Cajamarca, to your land to eat granadillas and chirimoyas [custard apples]," she replied sarcastically.

"You are always reminding me that I am not from Ferreñafe."

Manuel was a native of Chota who had resided since 1925 in Ferreñafe. He was a very attentive and cordial man whose manner of speaking easily revealed his mountain origin and ancestry. Most people knew him as "Topiquero."

This man played an important role and his services were in great demand. He was almost a social welfare institution for the people of that zone, where almost everything was cured with herbs — colic, hemorrhages, aches and pains, diarrhea, sprains, rashes, intoxications, and indigestion. His services were mostly free. Like a nurse and pharmacist, he could prescribe syrups, poultices, pills, lozenges, and capsules, and he could give injections. Some ladies used to say that he had a soft hand. He also functioned as a dentist, but not a painless one. In those days, extracting teeth was painful because there was no anesthesia.

Slowly the truck "Don Juan" began its march as the passengers accommodated themselves on their improvised seats. Some residents of the Alameda neighborhood raised their arms to wave goodbye to the travelers. The wading birds that nested in the tall ficus plants screeched and fluttered around the beautiful trees.

Suddenly something happened near the bridge in front of the house of a lady whom everyone called "Tortolita" [Turtle Dove] because of her short stature and the way she swayed as she walked. Many curious people made a circle around a person who was on the ground wallowing in agony.

"What's happening? Is it a fight among boys?"

"No...! It's 'Pelusa,' the young boy reared by Don Manuel. Always he's getting his 'Manuelitos.' Thank God it happened outside the ditch because if not, he would have drowned," commented a laborer who was carrying a saddlebag on his shoulder.

Pelusa did extreme contortions, his eyes were bulging, his arms were stiff, and foam sprouted from his mouth. He had epilepsy, a serious and almost incurable illness.

A lady was screaming wildly: "Leave space, open up, the boy needs air."

Then someone took off his reed hat and used it as a fan. The lady who was shouting crouched down, took the hand of the epileptic, then grabbed his middle finger and pulled it hard.

"That is the finger of the heart and it will calm his pain," she said.

"Poor boy," murmured a woman who was a pastry maker.

The truck "Don Juan" had its motor running, but the curious people would not move until they saw the conclusion of this unpleasant occurrence.

"It already happened!" Barbón said. "Come on, come on, get back onboard, the hours are passing."

When Pelusa recuperated, he looked at all the people around him, put his hand in his pocket, removed a piece of biscuit, bit it, and went walking among the ficus plants of the alameda, which had witnessed so many strange events that occurred there.

The Sights Along the Way

All the passengers made the sign of the cross as they passed the chapel with the image of Señor de la Justicia, whose festivities were carried out from the 23rd to the 27th of April. At the end of the alameda, the façade of the Virgen del Carmen cemetery stood out prominently. To one side of a small brick bridge some vaults of a very old cemetery could be seen.

"And what happens there? Do they no longer use those vaults?" asked a lady.

"Not anymore," answered Don Sevilla. "Only five Chinese citizens have been buried in this cemetery."

"Now where do they bury them?"

"There is no one to bury, Señora. The Chinese die old and that only happens every hundred years."

The rainwater had filled to capacity the so-called Flautero pit, also known as the pit of the drowned ones.

The wind agitated the wild reeds and rushes. The guinea fowl, ducks, and coots took to flight, frightened by the noisy motor of the old truck. A small fox crossed the road in the direction of a winter habitat of the white chisco [Mockingbird].

"Do you know this winter place?" Topiquero asked Tía Vige.

"What a foolish question you ask me if I am of Ferreñafe. I was born in this land where my bones will someday rest. I even know the owner because he is my neighbor. His house in town is close to mine on San Martín Street."

"But Tía Vige, do you know what happens in those winter habitats?" Manuel continued asking.

"What do you mean, thin dog?" Cholo's aunt inquired.

"Ah…! You see, in these winter habitats there exists an earthly paradise."

"Well, What I know is that on those lands are algarrobo trees and weeping willows. There are many nests of doves and in the highest branches hang enormous hives filled with honey."

"No, it's not just that. There's something else," replied Topiquero. "In those lands are many tame donkeys. This is the reason the young boys of the town go to this place each weekend. It's because there they can get their first sexual experiences."

"Oh … you stupid man! Then you must have been weaned there," the good seamstress said.

"Me? I'm not from Ferreñafe." Looking askance at Cholo, who appeared unworried as he held his slingshot, Topiquero said with sarcasm, "Aunt, you should take more care with your nephew. Many people have seen him patrolling those lands of Señor Mendoza."

21

"Shut up! My Cholo still is too young; he hasn't even smelled the skirt yet." She coughed three times and then stayed quiet.

Following the tracks left by other vehicles, "Don Juan" continued its march. The sand and clay did not allow the truck to go faster.

Scanning the panorama of that zone, the beautiful sown land cheered the spirit. Farm workers protected by wide-brim hats made of reeds were passing by mounted on their donkeys carrying pickaxes, rakes, machetes, and saddlebags. The solar rays were toasting the skin of their arms. The smiling faces of the ferreñafanos and the happy songs of the dark-plumed thrush were bucolic brush strokes that conveyed love and hope. The wind took charge of carrying them very far away.

Like white-handkerchief peace signs, white herons crossed the space. The sun was stronger, but a cool breeze announced the presence of the gigantic masses of stone that encircle the mysterious and prodigious lands of Batán Grande. It is there where fantastic treasures sleep, the inheritance of our ancestors; where characters such as Tungula, holding the hand of some god of the universe, built the incredible country of Sicán, where the moon sleeps and the sun cries.

Cheerful are those roads from Ferreñafe to Batán Grande. There to the right is the road to Nerio and Guanabal, further ahead are the irrigated lands of La Cruz del Caminante, La Pared,

El Rastrojo, Las Dos Puertas, and Jabonero. During those days, some of the more advanced small farms showed little flags of rice in the furrows of the dark land, the land of Santa Lucía.

The passengers who traveled in the cab were surprised by the cheerful singing of some peasants from the mountains. These were huaynito melodies with verses in Quechua. Dark red ponchos and straight, greasy hair identified those travelers on the roof of the truck as the original people of Ferreñafe and the legitimate heirs to the great fortune that Sicán keeps.

The secondhand hats worn by these young serranos [people of the mountains] were products of bartering. To obtain those items from the coast, they delivered excellent cheeses made with the milk of cows raised in the pastures of Mollán, Laquipampa, and Sangana. Some landlords who exploited these places had land titles of murky provenance.

In the settlement called Pítipo, two people awaited a lift from "Don Juan." They climbed to the top of the truck as Barbón climbed down. He went to a small tavern where he delivered two letters. As payment for his graciousness, the tavern owner presented him with a mug full of yonque. On his return to the wheel, the driver belched in a disgusting way. All who traveled next to him looked at him with anger, but he ignored them, lit a cigarette, and continued driving.

The cab was impregnated with the smell of alcohol. The smoke of the cigarette bothered Cholo, who stared at the smoker.

From above arrived the serrano singing. Those of the dark red ponchos continued to intone their chuscadas [traditional songs]. It was then that Barbón, perhaps stimulated by the yonque, began to sing a sad lambayecano whose lyrics belong to the poet from Chiclayo, Don Arturo Shutt Saco, and is still heard on some occasions.

The Chongoyapana

If because you have new loves,
you don't want me anymore Chongoyapana.

I also have somebody who dies for me,
my chiclayana.

Like the stones of Raca Rumy,
your soul is hard.

I also have somebody who dies for me,
my chiclayana.

I don't care that you don't want me,
Chongoyapana.

I also have other loves,
to forget you.

But I cannot because I live
seeing you ungrateful.

CHAPTER TWO

Crossing the Famous Zanjón

When they arrived at Mauro Bridge, an old structure of iron built over the so-called Loco River, the images of trees were dissolving into another landscape — rocky old roads where herders prodded their burros loaded with stones from the hills for the foundations of houses. Also went mules and horses, the saddlebags full of dreams.

As they passed near a mound of gray land, a redheaded vulture hastily devoured the corpse of a putrefied quadruped. The scraps were disputed. Just beyond, next to some wilted prickly pear cacti, two ravens smoothed their beaks on their strong wings; those birds of prey expected without any doubt to have a great banquet.

The heat was suffocating. Pooled water was starting to decompose. The famous zanjón was not yet visible. Owing to the intense heat, an almost imperceptible vapor emerged from the Batán

Grande soil. The motor of the old "Don Juan" was overheating. For that reason, Barbón decided to make another stop.

"Let's put some water in the radiator," the driver told Patuco. The assistant took a can and went in search of the liquid element. He was quick and returned in a few minutes, but he had to wait for the radiator to cool before filling it with water.

The gravel on the road was like the embers of a fire. The passengers were impatient to arrive at the estate.

The Competition

Tía Vige broke the silence and although she was somewhat lethargic from the trip, she asked Topiquero, "Thin dog, what are you going to do at the estate; are you healing someone?"

"No, aunt. This time it's one of the relatives of the estate's owners. The patient has dropsy. I take care of removing the liquid and then give him his injections."

"But the dropsy is not cured with injections," said the good seamstress.

"No! It's cured with cañazo [sugarcane liquor] and culen leaves," the man from Cajamarca said in a derisive tone.

"Stupid, for your information there are some herbs I know that are sufficient with three doses to cure that illness."

"Really? Please aunt, tell me what are these magic herbs. I will pay you very well if you tell me how and where I can obtain them. My patient has lots of money; he will pay with gold."

"Okay, killer of healthy people. When we get to the estate, I will take you to the house of a person who cures rare illnesses only with these miraculous herbs.

Tía Vige was well known for her curiosity. She knew how to prepare ointments, poultices, and water to cure frights. And, she could suture injuries. Above all, she was very successful curing innocent children who had been afflicted by mal de ojo [evil eye]. She also could remove the chucaque [spirits or traumas] that caused intense headaches and stomach pains. To cure her patients, she would pull a strand of their hair and she spit cañazo on it, and that was it.

"Aunt, for the diarrhea, what herbs do you use?"

"Oh, you mountain boy from the backwoods, doctors like you don't know anything; you have to learn from the women of Ñafe. Look, you obtain the shell of the coconut, boil it, add three leaves of plantain and five drops of lemon, and the illness is finished."

Tía Vige also could cure the fright of the dead and illnesses of the heart. For those ailments she prescribed cooking lemon balm and pimpernel.

Her prestige grew even more when the people discovered that this good lady cured out of neighborly love; she never charged a cent. That's why she lived modestly thanks to her work as a seamstress.

The Zanjón, the Zanjón!

At that precise instant a voice was heard shouting with great emphasis: the zanjón, the zanjón…! Already, everyone glimpsed what all expected to see. The zanjón, a huge water-filled gulch, was in sight. A strong wind was shaking the surrounding grove. During the rainy season it was dangerous to cross. The water was muddy and deep enough in many places to swallow a truck. When the passengers arrived at the edge, they all exclaimed at the same time: "It's completely full!"

The zanjón was a large, bowl-shaped depression formed when the waters of the remembered Loco River overflowed in the year 1925. It was a fatal time of torrential rains that whipped the entire northern part of Peru, causing irreparable damage from flash floods that ruptured channels and rivers.

A brown-haired lady who was wearing a flowered blouse and had around her neck a heavy gold chain with a wooden cross asked Barbón, "Señor, will we make it to the other side?"

"Look Señora," the driver answered, "this little truck you see here is capable of many feats. 'Don Juan' has a mind of its own that only lacks the ability to say: 'I'm screwed, but not defeated.'"

All of the passengers climbed down from the truck. Patuco already knew the routine and went to obtain dry branches, sacks, rocks, and lumber. With this they would improvise a kind of small bridge so that the vehicle could ford the pit.

After taking a good look around and probing the depth of the water, Barbón thought he had found a shallow place to try crossing. The passengers climbed back up on the truck as the driver's assistant waded warily into the dark water filling holes with the material he had collected. Almost all of the passengers entrusted their lives to their miraculous saints.

Tía Vige was nervous. She caressed Cholo and prayed thinking of the Holy Cross of Motupe as they initiated the crossing. Meter by meter they advanced toward the other shore. There was a moment of suspense when the old Ford of the year '29 wobbled, giving the impression that it would tip over. The skill of the driver avoided what would have been a tragedy for the more than twenty passengers who were eager to reach the land of the famous Tungula, creator of the incomparable whistling huacos.

A Respite Follows the Miracle

Everyone was ecstatic when they finally arrived at the opposite side. They thanked God for the miracle. Just then a loud bang was heard. It was the inner tube of the front wheel. The rubber tire had blown from the heat, the weight, and the years of use.

The wild birds that nested in the trees were frightened by the noise and took flight in terror. The zanjón was a bucolic place. A beautiful forest embraced that pit. One could breathe fresh air and perceive the fragrance of the flowers.

The sun's rays illuminated the nests of songbirds among the

branches of the algarrobo trees, and the wind wobbled the huge hives full of rich honey for the poor.

After a good while, multicolored butterflies arrived to the shore and kissed the flowers of the willow trees. A concert of wild birds welcomed the visitors who were traveling from Ferreñafe to Batán Grande.

All wished to do business there, so they could bring daily bread to their children who were looking forward to the return of their mothers and fathers, like the doves that carry in their beaks small branches, fruits, or nourishment.

Cholo took advantage of this uncertain moment to take out his slingshot and head toward a small grove where he heard the warbling of chiroques, chiscos, magpies, tordos, and chilalos. He knew that among those branches were nests with baby doves.

Meanwhile, as the poor Patuco removed the inner tube from the rim to patch it, someone asked him, "Hey, does the inner tube have holes?"

"This tire has more holes than the Merced tomb," the assistant answered without hesitation.

The zanjón was a rural property where many families lived and the men worked in the sown fields of the estate. They also sowed their own small parcels of land. They did not lack for good yucas, sweet potatoes, and corn. They also had fruit-bearing trees. Water never failed to irrigate their fields. The housewives raised poultry by feeding them corn, chopped carob seeds, and ground sweet potatoes. The turkeys of the zanjón were famous for being fat, large, and well fed.

Tía Vige was well known here because she always stopped on her way to the estate to offer her modest creations. Not in vain she spent entire nights in her house in Ferreñafe peddling her Pfaff machine, on which she sewed dresses, blouses, wedding gowns, shirts, and pants for children. The good aunt sacrificed herself to the extreme. She never complained about bad economic situations. When her sister Tarcila passed away, she took charge of five nieces and nephews. With her sewing machine, needle, thread, scissors, and lungs she managed to take care of five orphans.

A Cure for the 'Evil Eye'

"Doña Inés! Doña Inés!" the aunt called out several times. No one answered, but behind the door a pitiful crying of some creature could be heard. The shrieks were ceaseless.

A dog started barking. The animal apparently was made nervous by the presence of the strange visitor. Doña Vige tried calling out again with more force in her voice.

"Wait! I'm coming," the owner of the house said. "Please come in Señora Virginia."

"And the dog?"

"It only barks, nothing more. It's as docile as a man who is maintained by a woman," answered Doña Inés.

The visitor took a look around and called out for Cholo. He was busy harassing lizards and capons, and trying at the same time to catch a little dove with a broken wing.

"Cholo! Come here and hurry up!" his aunt shouted.

The little house of Señora Inés was very welcoming. It had a pretty patio with colorful flowers that grew in brown clay pots. The ceiling of the rustic house was made of hinea. Enormous bluebell flowers decorated the brass door. The fragrance of jasmine intoxicated with the perfume of springtime.

The ladies hugged each other. Tía Vige looked suspiciously at the shaggy dog that was still growling.

"What happened Señora Vige. Did the truck get stuck in the zanjón?"

"No, Doña Inés. A tire burst and now they are trying to patch it. The poor tire is like my slippers that are totally worn out from constant use."

"Who is crying in that manner, Señora Inés?"

"It's my zambita. Since dawn she has not let me close my eyes. My poor little girl screams and touches her belly. She opens her arms as if she is asking me something, but I have no idea what it could be. Is there anything I can give her?"

"Let's see. Bring her here."

The seamstress opened her old handbag where she kept the image of San Judas Tadeo.

Inés returned with her daughter in her arms. The girl complained more. Her crying was pitiful and worrying.

The visitor put the little girl on her lap face up and lifted her skirt. Touching the girl's abdomen, she exclaimed, "It's the mal de ojo [evil eye]!"

"Please bring me a fresh chicken egg. If it is from today and of a black hen, that would be much better. I'll remove the evil just with the hand."

The mother of the crying girl called to Coqui, her second child, and ordered him to go to the neighbor Andrea. There he was to ask for a fresh egg of the black hen that Tía Vige had requested. The boy went running and returned quickly.

"Mother, your comadre says these eggs are from this morning. The white one was laid by the little black hen and the green one by the one with an ashen comb.

The aunt took them in her hands and put the green one aside. With the white egg she began to rub the body of the little girl from head to toe. God only knows what prayers the good seamstress was murmuring. Almost instantly the patient stopped complaining. The screams ceased and after a while the girl went to sleep.

"It was the mal de ojo as I told you, Señora Inés."

"Malena, the daughter of my comadre Andrea, is responsible. When she came to visit me, my zambita was very cute. I didn't know the young woman had such a strong eye.

The seamstress broke the egg on the edge of a glass and placed its contents in the crystal-clear water.

"Here you can see clearly. If I had not arrived on time, I don't know what could have happened to your little girl."

Doña Inés took her daughter in her arms and carried the girl to the bedroom. Then both ladies began a pleasant conversation. The sky was gray in the land of Tungula.

"Señora Inés, where is your husband?"

"Santos left at dawn to go to the estate. Tomorrow is the fortnight's payday. I hope he brings money. The children must go back to school. We need to pay their registrations and buy their uniforms and notebooks. We also need to get many other things for the house."

"Just in case, you need to know that I carry small dresses and skirts, and pants that will fit Coqui."

"Oh, Señora Vige, you are such a nice person, but I don't want to abuse your generosity. Let's do this. If you don't sell some of your clothes at the estate, we can make a deal when you come back this way."

Already it was afternoon. Cholo asked for a glass of fresh water. The sun was burning and the heat was annoying.

"Señora Vige, can Cholo drink chicha?"

"Give it to him. That way he starts becoming a man."

"It's fresh. By Wednesday it will be very strong. I've prepared this chicha for the birthday of my Santos. For sure, friends and family will come. Last year they caught us by surprise. All our godparents arrived from the port of Eten. They brought a harpist and a singer who also was fantastic playing the drum. I wish you could come this year to learn the baile de tierra. I know my Santos is going to have a big celebration. He has uncovered an ancient tomb that he says has lots of rich items and all from the time of Tungula."

"Well, dear lady, for you I would come from Ferreñafe mounted on a donkey. But even though I die for enjoying the good chola music, this year I cannot dance. I have promised to keep two years of mourning for my sister Tarcila who died last year on April 10."

"The chicha is delicious," said Cholo as he drank from a little cup. The liquor was made from red corn sweetened with a syrup of dark brown sugar and cane sugar.

Beautiful white geese and native ducks were swimming in the zanjón.

"Look Señora, those ducks that you see over there are mine. I will cook them for the birthday of my Santos. In the corral I have two goats. There will be plenty of yonque. Already my Santos has ordered a container of cañazo from the distilleries in Mollán."

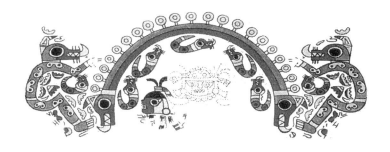

CHAPTER THREE

The Whistling Huacos

Cholo was entranced contemplating a huaco [ceramic] that was tied to a string hanging from a beam of the ceiling. When Doña Inés saw the great interest that the boy was showing in the clay object, she asked, "Do you like it?"

"Yes, it's very pretty," answered Cholo.

Señora Inés was a slender young woman with coppery skin, curly hair, and lively black eyes. Her voice was mildly hoarse.

She climbed up on an empty saddlebag, untied the huaquito [small ceramic], and gave it to the boy saying: "Cholo, this is my gift to you. Now it's yours."

That huaquito had as an allegory two tiny heads of foxes with eyes wide open. The small foxes were truly captivating.

Cholo thanked the lady for the gift with a spontaneous smile. That's when he remembered seeing a huaquito of a similar color and size at the home of his schoolteacher, Señor Martínez, in

Ferreñafe. That huaquito had three small foxes. The boys of the school used to play with it and were delighted with the musical sound that emitted from that piece of baked clay. Without doubt it was a whistler.

Cholo caressed his huaquito. He wanted to remove the coating of dust with a damp cloth, but Señora Inés would not allow it.

"You can never get this huaquito wet. It is a whistling huaco and if it gets wet, it will lose the beautiful sound it carries inside."

Tía Vige thanked Señora Inés for the gift she had given to Cholo. While both ladies were conversing, Cholo took the huaquito with love and brought it to his lips with the intention of kissing it. Without thinking he blew it with force and something unusual happened at that instant.

From that little piece of baked clay emerged a very sonorous sound that for some unknown reason disturbed the dogs. They began to howl pitifully and the chilalo birds started to sing their sad songs.

"Thank you for the gift Señora Inés. It has a beautiful sound. My Cholo will take good care of it. By the way, where did you find this whistling huaco? Is it from the Lucía tomb?"

"Look, Doña Vige, you know that my husband Santos is a tomb robber. He found it in an unknown tomb near Pomac. There were three related whistling huacos of the same size and color. The only difference is what you see here. The one I've given

Cholo has two little heads of foxes. The huaquito with three foxes Santos forgot at a tavern in the New Town of Ferreñafe."

"And the other one?" Cholo's aunt inquired.

"Oh lady, necessity has the face of a heretic. My Santos needed money, so he sold it to the herbalist from the jungle who lives at the estate. They say he is now a great shaman and they call him 'Timoteo.' Some people say this man has lots of money. Everyone believes in his powers. What few know is that the most important arte [magical objects] he has in his mesa [altar of sorcery] is a whistling huaco; the very one that is the brother of the huaquito your nephew Cholo is taking with him.

"What must you be thinking of me Señora Vige that I didn't invite you anything to eat? With the problems of my zambita, I didn't have time to start a fire in the hearth."

"Don't worry," answered the seamstress. "I always travel well covered. The same goes for my Cholo because he is such a glutton.

"Cholo, check to see if they have patched the tire. The sun is setting to the left, already it's after one o'clock."

While Cholo went to the place where the famous "Don Juan" was recuperating, the two friends continued talking. Suddenly the conversation took an unexpected twist.

In those days, news was circulating in the department of Lambayeque that tomb robbers were plundering the ancient graves and that at Batán Grande, in the place called Sicán, they had found rich treasures from pre-Inca cultures. They had discovered the mummies of leaders who once ruled those lands and there, almost on the surface, everything of value was exposed — jugs, vases, seashells, conches, trousseaus of gold, crowns, pectorals, bracelets, necklaces, precious stones of many colors, weaving of wool, even dark red corn cobs, and of course the incomparable huacos of clay.

The Strange Occurrence

"You're not going to believe what I will tell you. Ay!... Señora Vige, it may seem as if I am lying," Doña Inés said. It was the night of Good Friday. You know that the Holy Week is the perfect time to dig in the ancient tombs. People say that's when the spirits abandon their graves to wander and leave their buried possessions unprotected. So, during those days, the tomb robbers like my Santos feel safe to hunt for the treasures and remove them. My comadre Andrea is one of the witnesses to the story I am about to tell you. My older sister Estela who now lives in Patapo and two paisanitos who came from the highlands that night also can verify what I will tell you."

The paisanitos were from Penachí, the land of our brave ancestors who according to our history were never conquered by the Incas. Even today, these heirs of that lineage maintain their customs and beliefs. They wear dark red ponchos with black trimming as symbols of the royal blood of that indomitable tribe.

"We often gave those young men lodging here. Even though they spoke Quechua and barely could chew some Spanish, we were able to understand each other." Doña Inés continued, "On this night, they told of a rumor they had heard that tomb robbers had found an immense archaeological treasure in a pyramid near the estate. In Batán Grande, people only spoke of finding gold tumis [ceremonial knives]."

"So, what happened?" asked the visitor.

"Oh, I believe that God punished us. We had drunk many cups of top-quality yonque. You know that those days are sacred, but we continued guzzling the liquor. When we were in the midst of our drunkenness, Santos decided to bring out the whistling huaquitos he had found."

"Oh!… it's time to leave. Already they're sounding the horn." Tía Vige picked up her handbag, but before saying goodbye, being very interested in the story, she asked the owner of the house to continue with the narration. The aunt loved all tales of witches and mysteries. So, Doña Inés continued divulging the details of what had happened that night of Holy Week.

"Santos handed one of the huaquitos to my sister and the others to the paisanitos. Nobody could have anticipated what happened next. My husband ordered all of them to make the huaquitos whistle. Blow with all your strength, he told them. First, we heard a deep serious sound. Then a brighter but melodious sound emerged. All of them tried to get more sounds from the huaquitos they were holding in their hands. Suddenly, we heard a very clear and beautiful sound, almost like a lament. I asked myself, how is it possible that these small pieces of clay can produce such extraordinary musical notes?"

"And what happened then?" Tía Vige inquired.

"Oh Señora! An unexpected whirlwind agitated the water of the zanjón and all the birds in the corral cackled. While the music was coming from the whistling huacos, a moon of orange color appeared. There, among those hills you can see in front of us, thunder and lightning exploded. All the people who live here and in the surrounding areas panicked.

Perhaps intuitively, Santos snatched the huaquitos from the performers and put them in this saddlebag that I keep with me as a reminder of that strange occurrence. When we went to sleep that night, we were very frightened."

Tía Vige was used to hearing all sorts of strange tales, so she didn't give great importance to the story told by Señora Inés.

"Cholo, it's time to go. Say goodbye to the lady." So, the aunt and nephew walked to the truck. The motor was already running and again the passengers climbed onboard to travel to the town of the most fabulous estate in the department of Lambayeque.

The Enigma of Moisés

"Señor driver, do those fat animals belong to the estate?" a passenger asked.

"I think so Señora. They are worth a fortune, but not just the bulls, cows, and lambs. There's also a farm here where 'Moisés' has some huge young hogs of a special breed called Polanchín."

"Isn't it amazing what money can buy?" said the passenger.

All of the travelers in the front seats were looking with rapt attention at the immense grove they were about to enter and the road that now was made almost impassable by the large puddles.

"Then Moisés must have a lot of money. If he can handle all that and maybe the firewood and coal as well, he must feel like a king. It seems that God gave him plenty of everything."

"Not everything that shines is gold," added Tía Vige, who was following the conversation. "Life is an enigma. That man everyone is talking about was rescued from the zanjón. It was never known what malevolent mother put him in an empty basket wrapped in a dirty and frayed blanket and left him to the mercy of his luck. Two rural guards who by coincidence were passing by bound for Batán Grande and Sangana heard the pitiful crying of the unlucky boy and saved him from dying."

"And where did he end up? Surely at the estate house, no?" the passenger asked.

"The history is long and confused," Tía Vige answered. "I have visited this estate for more than ten years. During the 1925 rainstorms Moisés already was a young man. I always saw him mounted on his donkey carrying firewood, hay, and some fruits that the land gives.

"The people of this area say that Moisés had a star tattooed on his left arm. It was a mystery. Nobody knows why this muscular, dark-skinned worker appeared at the residence of a Japanese man named Tokomura."

"And doesn't he have a woman?" inquired the druggist. "Surely, he must have his partner hidden in some place. Men who live alone cannot be trusted."

And the tired "Don Juan" pressed on for the climb.

The Aunt's Remedy from the Trees

"Tía Vige, do you believe epilepsy is curable?"

"Well Señora, I know it can be cured if the patient is young, or better if he is a child. When the patient is an adult, the illness controls the person, so a cure is not possible. All is in vain."

"And how is it cured? What do you give to the patient?"

"Look, I don't know how to lie, but I have to tell you that I cured the son of one of my clients of this horrible disease."

"And with what remedy?"

"With something that many people do not believe is within reach of their hand. Pay attention because I will tell you this just once," the seamstress said as she divulged her remedy from the trees.

Just then a little bird with vermilion plumage arrived and began nibbling on small green branches. "That little bird we are watching is called a carpintero [woodpecker]. Their beaks are very strong. With it they can perforate the trunks of the trees to build their nests."

"How pretty!" the lady injected.

"The carpintero is a very restless little bird, but there are boys like my Cholo who hunt them in their nests."

"So, what are they good for?"

"Listen and hush up. When a person doesn't know something and wants to learn, he has to play stupid. All right," Tía Vige continued saying, "you open this little bird's chest and then you remove its heart and cut it crosswise with a shaving razor. The heart is put into a flask with sweet wine and when it has been marinated for seven days, you drink the wine. What I mean is that you give the patient a small glass every six hours."

"And the sick one gets cured?"

"Oh yes! All the nonsense goes away and the person stays healthy from then on."

Cholo was happy. While traveling he contemplated his huaquito and tenderly caressed the heads of the foxes. He thought about blowing the huaquito but then decided not to.

Along the road to Batán Grande, the passengers observed how a rancher, whip in hand, provoked a yoke of bulls trying to get them out of the mud. Further on could be seen beautiful horses in a corral surrounded by trunks of old trees; heaps of carobs attracted mosquitoes, the equines agitated their tails.

CHAPTER FOUR

The Welcome at the Estate

The entrance to the Batán Grande estate was very attractive. Laurels blooming in white and red, the national colors, gave the welcome. In the clear sky, flocks of mountain parrots crossed the space; their shouts could be clearly heard. Perhaps they were greeting the presence of the heroic "Don Juan" that had barely made it to his destination.

"The hours have wings! It's already past two in the afternoon," said Barbón to Patuco who had traveled the last stretch standing on the running board of the little truck. "As soon as we arrive, we'll go where is La Borrada. I could eat half a cow. My guts are growling, hunger doesn't wait."

Already in the town, the curious received with happiness the presence of the popular little truck, hero of so many expeditions. The sound of his motor betrayed him. The housewives greeted the conqueror of the zanjón; to cross it during those rainy days wasn't a game. On the main street of the estate next to the market, the old little truck was parked. The people of Batán Grande contemplated with admiration the popular and much beloved carriage. The rain had cleaned the sign that read "Don Juan."

The motor was switched off but it still discharged a hot vapor that was like the sigh of a human on his deathbed who had become used to saying: "I'm dying, but I'm not buried yet."

All the passengers took their belongings and went in search of their relatives or friends. Doña Vige said goodbye to Topiquero and made plans to get together the next day.

Cholo picked up the cardboard boxes. There in front of the small market was the house of the Gutiérrez family where the aunt lodged. Standing by the door of that welcoming home was Soledad, the second daughter of Don Carlos.

"What a pleasure it is to see you again Tía Vige. I knew you wouldn't be absent today. The reason? You already know it."

Soledad was a very attractive young woman with a white complexion, large eyes, distinct eyebrows, and long brown hair that fell to her waist.

"How pretty you are daughter. And how is my comadre?" the aunt inquired.

"She was invited to a lunch, but she will return in a few minutes. Please come in. This is your house.

In that home everything was in order. The furniture was covered with heavy fabric. In a picture frame at the center of a small table could be seen the smiling and happy faces of the spouses Gutiérrez Castilla. Don Carlos and Doña Elena appeared to have been in their twenties when the picture was taken.

High on a living room wall hung a beautiful painting of the sacred image of the Heart of Jesus.

"And my compadre?" Tía Vige inquired.

"He's in the administration office. He has many tasks to perform before payday, particularly with the laborers who work at the estate. Everyone can be absent except for my father."

As soon as the visitor installed herself in the bedroom, she washed her face in the basin. Her nephew did the same. The aunt and nephew gathered the boxes and excused themselves as they left the house in a hurry. "Soledad, I'll be back soon. I'm going to the forge. My clients are there."

"Go on Señora. Surely my mother will be here when you return."

A light wind and a chill wrapped the town. Dark clouds could be seen faraway in the mountains, but the sun was still shinning.

La Borrada's Kitchen at the Forge

"Cholo, hurry up! Leave that slingshot in peace. If we get delayed, we're not going to find anything to eat where La Borrada is cooking at the forge."

49

The estate house was there where the wide street ended. Two palm trees were rocked by the wind. The day laborers were making their way to the paymaster's office. Some were dressed in white shirts and pants. Others had their dark red ponchos and wore leather sandals. They carried saddlebags on their shoulders and machetes on their waists. Chewing their sorrows were these farmers of the fabulous land of Tungula.

The forge was the workshop where the estate's farm equipment was repaired. Damián, the master blacksmith, was a mulatto from Zaña. He was a mature man, but he was a very strong and happy person. Everyone in town knew him. In the very early hours, he could be found working at the furnace where he put the tips of plows in red-hot coals and gave form to many tools.

The blacksmith went by the nickname of "Lothar," a popular character of the comic strip "El Tony." Lothar was the faithful servant of the unforgettable Mandrake, the magician.

Lothar's neighbors were Teodosio and Rosaura from Illimani. Teodosio was retired from the army. His sister Rosaura was known as "La Borrada" [The Erased] because the cruel smallpox had left horrible pockmarks on the dark face of this provincial woman. She was a great cook who served delicious dishes at tables in the forge. She also prepared good chicha that she kept in large containers until she could bottle it.

The people of Batán Grande used to gossip a lot about Lothar and La Borrada. These two could understand each other in ways no one else could. Lothar was a master player of tejas. People would come to this town from faraway places just to compete in this game of skill that involved throwing metal discs on bricks.

Tía Vige and Cholo finally arrived to the forge and soon were savoring a well-seasoned bagre [catfish]. During the rainy season, bagres and other types of fish were abundant in the river.

"Teodosio," Tía Vige said. "I will leave this package with the brassiere your sister Rosaura asked for. Tell her that I will come back tomorrow. I have to visit other clients.

The sun went into hiding as clouds full of water began marching across the sky. The distant thunder and lightning were evidence that the rain would pour from jugs that night.

"It looks like it's going to rain," the aunt observed. "We should return to the home of my comadre Elena. I don't want to get caught in the rain. I could get a bad cold. I'm still recuperating from a strong flu."

The rain began falling just as they arrived at the house. Doña Elena was already there. Don Carlos caressed the hair of his daughter Soledad as Tía Vige was commenting on all that happened during the expedition of the fantastic little truck "Don Juan." Kerosene lamps and flashlights lit the house. In the kitchen a candle cried yellowish tears. The smoke impregnated the ceiling of old and oxidized calamines of zinc that bore the storm.

"Comadre Vige, did you know that this Sunday is the engagement party of my daughter Margarita?"

"Yes! It's a small town and huge hell. The news has wings and flies. I already know. Honestly, I don't remember the boyfriend. Have I met him?"

"Of course, comadre. He's the cocoa merchant who is called 'El Serrano.'"

"Oh! Evaristo. How is it possible, isn't that man married?"

"No. He has been with a Negro woman who has two small children. She lives at the Capote farm. But Evaristo is single."

It was very clear that Margarita's mother had already resigned herself to accepting the embarrassing situation.

"Comadre Elena. Is he the same serrano who has a child with a Negro woman in La Traposa? I think I also saw him there awhile back with an attractive serranita. Couldn't it be that…?"

She couldn't continue with more details because Doña Elena cut her off.

"Yes, I already know everything, but what can be done? Nobody can change the heart of a woman in love."

"It's a pity," Tía Vige said. "Margarita is much younger than he is. There is a proverb that says: 'The love and the interest went to a picnic one day. And more could the interest than the love she had.' How old is the boyfriend?"

"He's already passed 40."

"And my Margarita?"

"She will be 22 in the month of September."

"Well," replied the seamstress. "For love there is no age."

The owner of the house, who was somewhat tired after a long day, suggested to all, "We need to rest. Tomorrow we have to prepare the food for the guests who will be attending the engagement party on Sunday. We haven't invited many people, but we'll probably get lots of people passing by who want to enjoy a free meal."

As always on the last Friday of each month, the shaman Timoteo, who was a neighbor of Don Carlos and Doña Elena, was preparing to conduct his sessions of sorcery. Despite the rains, the pacientes [clients] were arriving protected by their blankets, ponchos, and reed hats.

The Mesa and the Language of Herbs

That night, while everyone slept in the house of the Gutiérrez Castilla, Timoteo prepared his potions. The herbs he boiled produced a sickening odor that inundated and contaminated the surrounding area, but his neighbors had become accustomed to the smell. Perhaps to remain on the sorcerer's good side, nobody dared to complain to the authorities of the estate.

Cholo tossed and turned in his bed, unable to sleep. His thoughts were fixed on the whistling huaquito, which he kept in a cardboard box under the bed of the good and loving aunt.

Already it was after midnight, the rain had ceased and the silence was almost total. Cholo rose to go to the corral. He had a need to urinate. As he was passing by the kitchen, a sad song accompanied by a kind of maraca caught his attention. He got up on the kitchen table and slowly approached the wall that abutted the house of the curandero [shaman]. Through a small opening he could observe some scenes that left him perplexed.

This was a session of witchcraft. Seated on dirty cushions, Timoteo sang and rattled his chunganas. At his side were people who drank a greenish liquid from glass cups. The alzadores [assistants] sipped through their nostrils a mixture of tobacco, yonque, and a powerful hallucinogenic herb called micha that is used in the sessions of curanderos.

In fan-shaped seashells they poured a liquid that was absorbed by the alzadores and some of the pacientes [patients]. When the sick ones began to dance to the rhythm of the chunganas, the rain started again but with much more force than before.

Cholo observed everything that was in the curandero's mesa. On a blanket laid out on the ground, he saw bottles of transparent glass that contained dissected snakes in alcohol, rusty sabers, daggers, rare stones, wilted flowers, and huacos of all forms, colors, and sizes. Also, there were paper prints with images of San Cipriano, shells, and snails on some small willow tables.

He could see other flasks with live herbs, necklaces of blue beads, a whip, and two crosses — one of stone and another of white wood. Rain, dances and strange songs, herbs, tobacco, and fragrances, that was the sorcery that existed in this region. These are ancient beliefs that are passed down from generation to generation throughout time.

A horrendous scream suddenly came from a young woman. Cholo trembled but he couldn't stop watching the spectacle. The young woman threw herself to the floor and began to shake like a poisoned dog. The alzadores sprinkled cañazo on her body.

Timoteo silenced his chunganas. Taking a branch of a quince tree, he cut the air with a slashing gesture.

A young woman continued in her delirium, saying incoherent things. The ones who were dancing with frenzy seemed not to realize what was happening.

A very young alzador approached the maestro Timoteo and whispered in his ear. The curandero sought a small box of carved wood, opened it, and extracted something that caught Cholo's attention. It was a huaco identical to his, the same color and size. That huaco was the greatest arte of the mesa handled by Timoteo, the most famous teacher of Sicán sorcery.

Timoteo lit four candles and burned the holy stick. Then taking a little bottle of cañanga water, he gave a drink to the woman who was convulsing. In the middle of the lit candles was the huaquito. That jewel was the same one that Señora Inés always lamented because the tomb robber Santos had sold it for almost nothing. Cholo was so full of emotion that he almost fell down from his perch. Timoteo drank something from a bluish flask that he spat in a fine spray on the huaquito. Then he brought it to his lips and blew with force. An extraordinary sound emerged instantly from that piece of baked clay.

The dancers became quiet and the young woman stopped screaming, the rain ceased and all remained in silence. Cholo climbed down from the table and hurried to the corral to relieve himself.

When he returned to his room he tried to sleep but couldn't. That mysterious melody, so similar to the one made by his little whistle, would not leave him in peace. Soon the song of the rooster could be heard, already it was almost dawn.

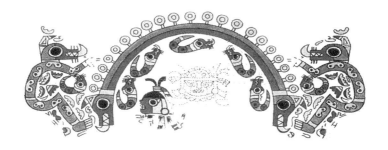

CHAPTER FIVE
An Early Start

On Saturday all awoke very early. The corral was mud. A servant girl swept the living room and dusted the furniture. In the oven made of adobe bricks burned the firewood that happily was kept for this day. At breakfast time all the family was seated around the table in the dining room.

Tía Vige took the pitcher of hot chocolate and muttered, "It's boiling, but that's the way I like it. This chocolate is delicious. I'm sure it must be from Mayascón."

"Where is Cholo?" Nicolás, the youngest son of Doña Elena, asked.

The aunt responded, "I guess the sheets have glued him to the bed and he's still asleep. I'm going to wake him up because we must go to several houses. My clients are awaiting me. I need to take advantage of the day to catch lots of fish."

"Agustina, put two tins of water to boil," Doña Elena ordered the servant. "The hours are flying. We need to slaughter the pig, clean it, season it, and put it in the oven. I hope Don Crispín lit his oven. Yesterday, I saw him at the tambo [small store]. He was drinking wine with that Topiquero who lives in Ferreñafe."

All was planned for Sunday, the day of the engagement party for Margarita, perhaps the daughter most spoiled by her parents. She was beautiful, tall, slender, and the owner of a prominent bust that was the admiration of many young men. Margarita took charge of cutting the necks of the chickens, ducks, and turkeys. The party would be lavish.

That Saturday morning the sun caressed the hills. In Batán Grande there was lots of activity; it was fortnight and everybody expected to be paid. From various locations the laborers arrived to the estate with mules carrying heavy loads.

The hour of truth was approaching. Almost everyone in the town was aware that on Sunday a lucky man would ask for the hand of Margarita. One of the Aurich brothers would be a witness to that commitment. Don Carlos was meditative but proud to know that an owner of the estate would do him that honor.

Meanwhile, the aunt and nephew carefully negotiated the muddy streets loaded with their merchandise, trying to sell enough to make ends meet. In Ferreñafe, the four orphans were awaiting the return of this sacrificing seamstress.

When the town of Batán Grande awoke on Sunday morning, all of the people were optimistic and happy. It was month's end and with money more cannot be requested, some said. The day laborers cleared their debts from the previous two weeks and again gathered provisions. Food was the first necessity but they also took stockings, garters, combs, powders, rouge, lipsticks, perfumes and other things.

The Party Begins

A fireworks display and lively music could be heard throughout the neighborhood of the estate house and in the old tambo of the property. Along the counter, the laborers were drinking. Then a bottle of yonque was only 50 centavos, sweet pastries were 10 centavos each, and a quarter container of Chinese rice was 40 centavos. The Japanese Nakasaki needed several hands to distribute the provisions. Always with his Faber pencil, he kept tabs for the next fortnight of the orders for noodles, canned tuna fish, vinegar, sugar, candles, and matches.

The sky was clear. Out on the main street, the people were witnessing something that is rarely seen. A hawk was pursuing a tender young dove. Both birds were zigzagging in space until the bird of prey finally trapped the little bird. A laborer from La Traposa exclaimed, "As soon as the hawk put his eye on the dove, it captured the soul of the other life! The dove could not escape its fate."

On that wide main street there were two barbershops run by Japanese. There a client asked Maeda, "What festival are they celebrating today?"

"I not know. Here always party, party, happy people."

Another client, who was waiting his turn for a haircut, exclaimed, "I believe it's a jarana [big party] at the estate house! The Grau band from Ferreñafe is there."

"Really! That band of negroes plays very well. But how did they get here if the zanjón is full to its ears?"

"They went around by way of Chiclayo," mentioned an old man. "The Aurichs have, and 'when you are rich, all is possible.' "

The Fatal Epidemic

Several clients of the forge eatery were commenting about the epidemic that was causing so much havoc in the region.

The bubonic plague was beginning to attack Lambayeque towns; the alarm was general. Already, it had caused deaths in Incahuasi, Mayascón, and La Traposa. Each day, the plague was coming closer to Batán Grande and Ferreñafe.

Tía Vige smiled with disdain and said, "More is the fear of what is said, than the damage caused by the illness! I know how and with what the bubonic is cured." She had in fact suffered from the plague and cured herself with a homemade remedy.

"Aunt," shouted one of the parishioners. "You better take the last drink because the plague is close by the zanjón."

"Then you better take care of yourself," the woman of Ferreñafe answered, "because the bubonic plague only gets you once, and if you don't die, then there's nothing to worry about. But just for your information, this plague is cured with the juice of the cucuno. This herb is much more bitter than the mother-in-law of a drunken womanizer like you know very well, but it cures. Also, it is good to rub the infected areas with iodine and Vaseline to reduce the swelling, and you have to disinfect the wounds with diluted phenol."

When Damián, the lover of La Borrada, heard what the aunt said, he downed a double drink of cañazo and, since he knew how to sing a cappella, intoned some verses that people sang to the rhythm of the baile de tierra.

"The blacksmith sings well!" said "Puche" Vilela. "Serve him more cañazo to see if it encourages him to sing us something from Chongoyape." Damián didn't wait for them to beg him to sing. He soaked his throat and intoned another sad song.

Meanwhile the forge was overwhelmed with clients. All came to taste the delicious dishes. Some of the customers would pass the day playing briscan [a Spanish card game], and throwing tejas on bricks marked with chalk.

Mounted on his spirited steed, "Cholo Lolo" did pirouettes in the middle of the street. The people knew that when that horse trader had too many drinks, he liked to show off.

Just then there passed by a funny dwarf called "Juanito" from an estate near Chiclayo. Dressed as an engineer, he wore a khaki-colored outfit, gaiters, and a helmet. That day he had tied around his neck a yellow silk scarf. In his right hand he carried a whip with a leather handle. The youngsters made fun of him, but the Lilliputian one just smiled and looked at them with disdain.

The aunt received some coins from the hand of La Borrada. Some business had been transacted.

"Do you think your brother Teodosio would be willing to give me a turkey on credit? I will pay him the next fortnight."

La Borrada answered her instantly, "Señora, the turkeys are mine, you can take one or two. Later we'll reach a deal."

"Then tomorrow morning I will come for them before I return to my land."

In the tambo worked Señor Cruz who was the right-hand man of the Japanese. This gentleman of Lambayeque controlled the notebooks of the debtors. On his ring finger he wore a huge ring of pure gold. When people asked him where the precious metal came from, Don Cruz responded with pride, "This gold is from the land of Tungula."

Back at the forge, Tía Vige put her hand into a paper bag, removed a pair of lace panties of a heavenly color and offered them to La Borrada.

"No, Señora. You don't owe me anything. I will never forget the time you cured me of my terrible stomach cramps. Ay, mamita! If it was not for you, I would not be recounting this story."

She tried to give back the intimate gift, but already the aunt was going out the door. She had to arrive on time for the engagement of the beautiful Margarita.

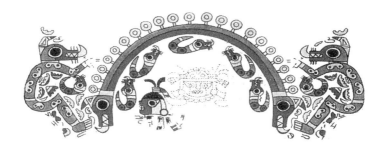

CHAPTER SIX

Marriage and Shroud Come from Heaven

In the Gutiérrez Castilla home, everybody was very busy. The hour was approaching and the guests were about to arrive. In the kitchen the cooks were sweating fat drops. The heat was a killer. The calamines were radiating heat from the burning sun and there almost was no air.

There was the large rectangular table, clean white tablecloths perfectly pressed, with trays of baked turkey, egg bread, black olives from Monsefú, and good mountain cheese. In pots of clay they had stewed ducks, salty mackerel, corn, and the best yucas of Batán Grande that had the softness of cotton. The banquet would be of top quality.

The first guest to arrive was "Blind Elías," a real maestro of the guitar. This great artist from Ferreñafe, who was blind from childhood, enjoyed great fame throughout the department of

Lambayeque. As soon as he arrived, they offered him something to eat and a cup of good yonque. The artist took out his guitar, his faithful companion, and began to perform classical works. Later he played pasacalles, tristes, valses, boleros, and marches.

Don Carlos was spellbound listening to him. Agile fingers slid on the neck of the guitar producing sonorous musical arpeggios that resembled the sounds of the cataracts, water falling pure and crystalline. Blind Elías was totally absorbed extracting beautiful cords from the six metallic strings.

Tremulous smooth notes invited dreaming. A sublime melody touched the most intimate fibers of the human being. Never before had anyone played a guitar in such a way in that house. For that reason, all who listened to the magical sounds that poured from that Spanish instrument remained perplexed and then applauded the maestro. Don Carlos embraced the blind musician and begged him to play the Morán march. The artist complied and later played the works of other renowned composers.

"Maestro, maestro. Why don't you sing the baile de tierra that is so popular in all the department of Lambayeque, the one that says the priest Chumán charged quotas to the landowners?" A mature woman was the one who requested that song.

"With all due respect, Señora, I know that song. Please don't forget that I just sang 'The 300 Pounds of Gold.' I'm always ready to please my audience with available material."

After several cups of yonque, the baile de tierra gave happiness to the hearts of all the guests who looked forward to the engagement of the beautiful Margarita.

"Maestro Elías, after the ceremony, when things have calmed down, I would like to listen to the pasillo of Ecuador, 'Black Flowers,' that says: 'Under the ruins of my passions....'"

"Don't worry Señora Emerita. I will please you, I won't forget your request." The guitarist hung up his instrument on a nail.

Hurried and agitated as always Tía Vige arrived. The first thing she did was to ask for the fiancée.

"Where is Margarita?"

"She's in her room," the younger sister said.

"Then excuse me, I'm going to comb her hair."

As the aunt was passing through the kitchen, the servant girl greeted her and after carefully examining her she said in a low voice, "I think you might be a little drunk."

"No...!" answered Cholo's aunt. "I only had a small glass of anis because my stomach hurt and I had a terrible headache from all the worrying."

Margarita had just finished dressing when the aunt entered her room.

"Hello Doña Vige. And how was your day?"

"Alright, thanks to my Cross of Motupe. Like they say: 'Dogs that walk, find bones.'"

Tía Vige combed the fiancée's hair and left quickly for the street with the intention of greeting the compatriots of her husband Don Kanno: Goto, Tokomura, and Maeda, workers at the estate who had been invited to the social event of this day.

There in the barbershop of the Japanese Maeda, the compatriots were gathered. The aunt was conversing with all of them when they heard the sound of a small flute and the tam-tam of a little drum. He was a Chilico who carried the image of the Virgen Peregrina [Wandering Virgin] in a tiny glass case. He asked for alms and the people who adored [the Virgin and contributed a few coins] received a small piece of blessed cotton.

"Where are you from?" asked the seamstress from Ferreñafe.

"I am from Celendín," the flute player answered.

"Ah! Then you are from the land of the lying Topiquero."

The Japanese, who were neighbors of Don Carlos, groomed themselves in front of the mirror. All were invited to witness the engagement of Margarita. The estate house was not far from the house of Don Carlos. The wind carried the happy notes played by the Grau band. This musical group was rehearsing. It would be a surprise to Margarita from the patrón [property owner]. The band would enliven the ceremony and fill the neighborhood with joy.

The Arrival of El Gringo Jaime

"Look who just arrived!" It was the cook who announced the presence of Jaime, a popular character in Batán Grande. Most knew him as "El Gringo." Actually, he was an American born in Oklahoma, but that was not known until a long time later.

Jaime said he worked as a technician for one of the largest oil refineries in the United States of North America. He was a tall young man with white skin and hair the color of carrots. His dense and long beard gave him a more adult appearance.

Jaime almost always arrived in town, mainly on paydays, carrying a leather bag. He dressed modestly in corduroy pants, checkered shirt, cloth hat, and high boots. He wore glasses with tinted lenses, smoked cigarettes with a mouthpiece, and drank only a little alcohol.

He made his living by getting unwary people to sell him precious metals at bargain prices or by bartering. Jaime brought lots of trinkets for women, which he exchanged for items found in the [pre-Columbian] tombs. He often could be seen testing the purity of the gold he acquired by means of the acid he poured from a small crystal container kept in his bag.

"Señor Jaime, I have two very pretty huaquitos. Don't you want to see them?" a guest inquired.

"Are they whistlers?"

"No, but they have the forms of an owl and a toad."

"Good, I want to see them. If I like them, we can make an exchange."

From a corner of the living room, another person called to the gringo. "Come here Jaime. Please have a seat next to me. I'm very glad to see you." He was an agent of the civil guard who arrived once in a while to keep order in that town.

The Hand of Margarita

"This wine is very good! Is it from an earthen jug?" It was Blind Elías who was savoring the nectar of the grape.

"You have a good palate, maestro. Nothing but the best for the best."

"You can say whatever you want, but I can tell this is an excellent wine from Jayanca. Nobody deceives me."

The other guests were accommodating themselves. The living room seemed to be getting smaller.

"He's coming! He's coming!" shouted a girl who was by the door. All the guests stood up to receive the happy mortal who only God knew how he had conquered the heart of the beautiful Margarita.

Evaristo crossed the middle of the street dressed in beige pants, a poplin shirt, and a palm hat with a wide brim. He had gold rings on his fingers and a varnished leather band around his wrist. At his side walked his sister Candelaria, a woman of bad temper and ignorance. She barely could sign her name, but she was a very hard worker dedicated to the business of yonque, cocoa, and salt.

Candelaria was wearing a new satin dress the color of the sky and black high-heeled shoes. On her shoulder she carried a large leather purse with butterfly clasps.

Behind the couple, a boy mounted on a donkey with wide saddlebags held two beautiful peacocks. This was Evaristo's gift to his future in-laws, Carlos and Elena.

Evaristo had taken the arm of his sister Candelaria. When he arrived to the house, he removed his hat, greeted all the guests, and embraced his future father-in-law. The brother and sister were warmly received.

In the bedroom, Margarita was very nervous. Doña Elena was helping her put on a pair of delicate pearl earrings when she said, "El Serrano has arrived with his ill-tempered sister."

Evaristo had a great facility for words and expressed the motive for his visit. The parents formally presented Margarita and at that moment the Grau band began playing a happy polka. This was the gift from one of the Aurich's to the most beautiful and admired young woman in all the estate.

While the people of this small town enjoyed the music, in the house the friends of Margarita looked sad when she accepted Evaristo's proposal. All of them wished for Margarita someone better. She was so pretty, so industrious, and so young; but as the proverb says: "In life when someone proposes, another disposes, then the devil arrives and all decomposes."

By all accounts the celebration was a great success. "Events like this just don't happen every day," commented the people of the town. "Long live the bride and groom! Now dance and kiss!" everyone shouted.

The guests were enjoying that happy afternoon because when love arrives, sadness must leave. Exquisite dishes of native food paraded one after another. Then came the wine, the beer, even unknown liquors that were the delight of the guests.

Candelaria was feeling slightly drunk when she left her seat and in an act of wanting to challenge the patrón, she approached the witness and invited him to dance a huaynito. Without further ado, almost disrespectfully, she took him by the arm and pulled him toward the street. On their way out the door, she ordered the band to play the Silulo, a carnival dance from Cajamarca.

When all the instruments had marked the beat of the huaynito, Don Juan Chico started with his bombo and soon the trumpets, saxophones, and clarinets harmonized in the melody that was so Peruvian and so popular.

What the stubborn Candelaria had not imagined is that the patrón could dance the huaynito with style and grace because in his blood ran the blood of Batán Grande.

The patrón and Candelaria received a loud applause. The band immediately followed with "Adolorido," a fashionable song. Don Carlos recalled the lyrics: "I'm suffering, I'm suffering, I'm suffering in my heart, for an ungrateful one, for an ungrateful one who left a hole in my heart… ."

From somewhere Topiquero affirmed, "How well El Serrano dances."

"Of course, he's going to dance well if he's a regular client of the houses in the pleasure quarter of Chiclayo. I always see him there during the last days of each month. El Serrano has his money and he knows how to enjoy it," the agent of the civil guard said as he hurriedly gulped down the wine in his cup.

Perhaps exhausted by the celebration, Evaristo and his sister decided to leave. The afternoon was dark and it appeared that rain would return that night in all the region of Sicán.

While the people continued listening to the Grau band, Señora Elena ordered that they serve double portions to the musicians. "They deserve it," whispered Margarita's mother.

"Mamón", the group's triangle player, was wolfing down dish after dish. The guests admired his ability to devour so much food. He was known by that name in Ferreñafe because he suckled his mother's breasts until the incredible age of ten. As the night approached, some guests left without saying goodbye while others arrived with the intention of finishing off Sunday.

After the Band Stopped Playing

When the band finally stopped playing, it was time to retire and rest. The rain was imminent. There on the main street could be seen the mistreated little truck, alone, and abandoned to its luck. "Don Juan" seemed to say in a sad voice, "They only love me when they need me."

In the dining room, the most intimate friends of the family chatting animatedly. Blind Elías dozed peacefully in a hammock. In the living room, various guests who had imbibed more than a few too many drinks slept like monkeys.

The blacksmith Damián, who arrived late with a sugar cane worker, described the scene with a native expression: "There are more persons dead than alive, but the war continues."

There was no lack of gossiping about the betrothal and one guest dared to insinuate that perhaps Margarita had been bewitched by some curandero of that zone.

Another guest intervened in the conversation and promised that he would ask Timoteo to conduct a mesa to see if the girl had been the object of sorcery.

"Who is this person?" investigated Jaime.

"He is the teacher Timoteo, the one who shakes the chunganas and knows all with his herbs," assured a neighbor.

"Those beliefs are fairy tales. I don't believe in them," asserted Jaime.

"No? Look gringo, that man has a whistling huaco that when he blows it, the sound makes the ground tremble. I tell you this because I have witnessed it. The same story is told by Señora

Inés, the one who lives at the zanjón, and Tía Vige also knows. She's a friend of Santos, the famous tomb robber."

At that point of the commentaries almost all put their "spoon" [opinion] in the conversation. The meeting became more interesting when Don Maeda, "El Viejo" [The Old One] as people used to call him at the estate, dared to predict: "Someday will come from very far, perhaps from Japan, an expert archaeologist, and, with the aid of someone like us, he will discover the oldest and most important tomb of Batán Grande, the land of Sicán, cradle of Tungula."

Everyone ignored that Jaime had studied at a university and claimed to know a lot about the nuclear sciences. Yonque causes those who drink this hard liquor to speak, so two good cups loosened the tongue of the gringo.

"Now I remember," explained Jaime. "In the university where I studied a group of scientists were investigating the influences of color and sound on the human mind. By using special techniques and the extraordinary powers of color and sound, they were able to cure the sick with incredible results."

Continuing with the theory he had learned, he also said, "Each person has a color and a sound. When a person is sick, you must try little by little to balance them. That coincidence will alleviate the patient's illness in an instant. Perhaps this occurred many centuries ago when the alchemists were sure that the human body was just vibrations, that's to say music and harmony. The body seems to respond when it finds agreement with its color and sound."

Hardly anybody gave much credence to what was said by the gringo Jaime, who was trying to show off his knowledge.

"If the sound from a piece of baked clay could achieve this rare effect on the behavior of an unbalanced mind, it's logical to assume that music would have a great influence on humans." The gringo smiled, downed his glass of yonque, and looked for the most discreet way to establish a conversation with Tía Vige.

The Bewitching of the Whistling Huacos

It was raining, so everyone decided to stay under the roof of the house. Anyway, the conversation was very interesting, the wine was good, and so was the yonque. Don Carlos, a man who knew a great deal about the mysteries of that region, gave an exposition on Sicán and Tungula, the fantastic personage who is said to have had magical powers and possessed nearly all of the whistling huacos, which Mother Earth now keeps in her bowels in Batán Grande, the land of gold and dreams.

Suddenly, a sweet and vibrant melody invaded that part of the house. The drowsy guests seemed impelled by a strange force to jump up in their seats.

Then Timoteo, the shaman and neighbor who was present, listened intently and somewhat disturbed by the alcohol, the circumstances, and by the magical sound exclaimed: "It's a whistling huaco! Who is whistling at this hour?"

In an impertinent way he abandoned the living room and walked to the small room where the melody was originating. Tía Vige smiled and tried to disguise the fact that she knew it was her nephew who was causing that sound. Timoteo found Cholo caressing the wonderful whistling huaquito that Señora Inés had presented him.

"Oh… Good Lord! It's identical to the one I have," murmured the healer. Without saying another word, the healer left in a hurry, but returned almost instantly. He brought a little wooden box, the same one Cholo had seen that Friday night when Timoteo was curing the infirm ones.

The healer opened the little box in the presence of all the guests. Then he extracted his small and black huaco.

"This whistler is a brother of the one that Cholo is holding, only my huaco has four little heads of foxes and the one that we were listening to has only two.

And that's how all of them arrived to a very strange and confusing world. The fantasy caused deliriums and submerged them in captivating stories. The enchantment of that whistle was like a torch that illuminated the dark path where mankind walks ignorant of so many things. After the stories told by Don Carlos, none of the lingering guests were sleepy.

Jaime didn't waste time and looked for a way to start up a conversation with Tía Vige. The gringo was well aware of the seamstress's needy situation. That's why he was so sure of his ability to negotiate an exchange of the type he was accustomed to transacting.

The Japanese guests continued drinking and talking about the pre-Columbian Sicán tombs at Batán Grande. El Viejo Maeda seemed to have the most knowledge about the existence of the valuable treasures.

In those days, news circulated throughout the department that in the Pomac forest robbers had plundered some tombs. Mute witness to this was a thousand-year-old algarrobo tree called "Gacho" [Drooping], a symbol of the northern flora. The poet from Illimani Rómulo Paredes Gonzales said:

> *The algarrobo tree,*
> *the god that never cries.*
>
> *The algarrobo tree,*
> *the devil that never prays.*
>
> *It doesn't need anything,*
> *in its greatness.*
>
> *It never asks for anything,*
> *and never implores.*

Precisely in the land of Illimo, the tomb robbers had exhumed the famous golden tumis that belonged to the Sicán territory of Batán Grande. Everyone speculated that more than ten gold tumis were found in those years.

The sun was offering its first rays of the day Monday; clarity illuminated all of Batán Grande. The voice of the young cane worker broke the silence with the romantic verses of an old cumanana. Margarita was sleeping and maybe dreaming with her adored tormentor. The regal voice of the laborer awoke her. The timid and sleepy fiancée appeared from behind the curtains of her bedroom window and congratulated the singer. She left her room and offered him a glass of sweet chicha in gratitude.

"To the one who gives what she has, when she doesn't owe anything," offered Lothar. Then he begged the future bride to recite some of the poems she had written. Margarita was a romantic woman and kindly accepted the blacksmith's request. The trills of the little gorrion birds could be heard. A fresh drizzle wet the land as the verses were heard in the voice of the author:

> *Love of sun and moon,*
> *love of hill and water.*
>
> *That makes me strong and vital,*
> *protected by you and part of you.*
>
> *You are my friend, my lover, my very life,*
> *sweetness of all my days.*
>
> *Shelter from my sorrows,*
> *sedative of my pains.*
>
> *You are filling my mind*
> *with illusion and fantasy.*
>
> *My lips are pronouncing your name,*
> *you know how to understand me.*

And in this dawn,
you are in my thoughts.
And you are like the burning fire
that I feel inside of me.

The velvety and sweet voice of Margarita cooed like the doves of the field and awoke almost everyone. The father Don Carlos embraced his dear daughter, kissed her on the cheeks and in their eye brought forth tears of joy. The old man understood that love has no barriers.

The lady Elena was just waking up to the sound of so many verses and wistful melodies. The time had passed quickly without anyone noticing. Already it was the hour for breakfast. All took leave because it was Monday and they had obligations. Tía Vige went to La Borrada's place to gather the turkey that was promised to her.

The Missing Huacos

When Cholo awoke, he went in search of his whistling huaquito to caress it. He looked for it in the cardboard box and didn't find it. He was worried and questioned everyone in the house about his huaquito, but nobody could give him an answer. Some said they had never seen it. He cried hopelessly and counted the seconds until his aunt would return.

At the house of Don Carlos's neighbor, a similar situation was occurring. Timoteo also looked for his charm and the arte of his mesa, the precious whistling huaco, and could not find it.

He attempted to appear calm, but his wife knew him very well, and when he tried to lie down on the mattress, she interrogated him.

"Where is the whistle? At dawn you took it. Where have you left it? I hope it isn't going to be that you were drunk and lost it. That would be a disgrace."

Timoteo looked out of the corner of his eye at the nightstand where an alarm clock was marking time. The rhythmic tick tock brought him back to reality. He didn't need to be a sorcerer to realize that the swindler Jaime had taken his huaco.

"And how much did you pay for that clock with tin plating?"

Timoteo didn't answer. He thought about going in search of that cheater to give back the clock and demand the return of his huaco. His wife, who had anticipated his thoughts, told him, "That gringo con artist has already left for Ferreñafe in the truck that brought the band of musicians."

When Tía Vige returned to the house, Cholo tearfully asked her, "Where is my whistling huaquito?"

Pretending to be angry, the aunt answered, "You don't need a huaco. Anyway, it's just a piece of clay. Why do you want that nonsense? Aren't you happy with the toy made of orange wood that the gringo Jaime left for you?"

"Yes, I like the toy, but it doesn't whistle. The sound of my huaquito makes me dream beautiful things."

Cholo cried. His sadness was overwhelming. Nothing could be done. He would return to Ferreñafe with only his inseparable slingshot made of willow wood that he used to hunt little birds and lizards.

Epilogue

Time has neither memory nor voice. It's also deaf. It doesn't listen to pleas or utter words, but it conveys majesty and condemnation. Nearly 70 years have elapsed since that morning in 1937 when Aunt Virginia traveled with Cholo to Batán Grande. Now Cholo is almost an octogenarian, but he continues to daydream. His children took him to Japan, the land of his father. He cannot believe that he's traveling on the swift and modern shinkansen [bullet train]. When he is tasting hambagas and misoshiros, his palate longs for the flavor of his food seasoned with chili pepper and mint.

In Yokohama, Tokyo, or Nagoya, they no longer drive those little trucks from the year 1929. All has changed. Now man kills with thermal and atomic bombs. Television is the bread of the day. People already are preparing to build houses on the Moon. Japanese technology arrives in all the countries of the globe. The sound of the harp with cords of catgut are muted; now the

83

musical instruments are so sophisticated and cacophonous that they damage the eardrums.

Cholo walks slowly as he patrols the edge of an immense river. He enters a temple and bows before an unknown image. He prays and implores, but the image does not seem to understand; perhaps it ignores what he says. It's another country, another language, another reality.

His loving Aunt Virginia is no longer. The moon is hiding. Under the snow that falls in December the yuyo plant probably would grow in this granular and almost yellowish soil, but here there are no huacos from the land of Tungula. Cholo dreams of bracelets, crowns, and pectorals of fine metal. Japan is another world. Here silence lives. The huerequeque and chilalo birds don't sing. Absent is the magical sound of the whistling huacos.

El Canto Silvestre [The Sylvan Song]
Cumanana
Lyrics and Music: Luis Abelardo Núñez

The charm of Sicán
flourished in the year one thousand
from Illimo to Mollán,
said the song of the Til Til bird.

In the branches of a mamey
a cucula bird cried
at the death of the king
who was called Tungula.

*His noble wife Kalina
had a beautiful voice
like an Andean dove
and Tungula was her God.*

*A little parrot proclaimed
Tungula was born in the Ande.
A chiroque bird replied
his cradle was Batán Grande.*

*In Pomac, there are two hills,
one is the color of saffron.
where little foxes burrow
in the land of Sicán.*

*There is no place in Lambayeque
like Sicán with so much gold,
proclaimed the huerequeque,
and it's true the bull said.*

*Tungula, Tungula,
only you made things of beauty
that captured the sound
in your whistling huacos.*

*Juice of greenish plants
with leaves like passion fruit,
the rocky stones they dissolve
transforming them into clay.*

*This secret is known by the bee
that flies and buzzes.
Tungula knew the key
and took it to his tomb.*